THE ADVENTURES OF SAMMY THE SNOWFLAKE

The Facts of Life, Flying, and Finding Weather

By Brooke Becker
Illustrations by T. Kyle Gentry

Courtyard Publishing, LLC
Miami Beach, FL

Courtyard Publishing, LLC
Miami Beach, FL

Visit Sammy at www.sammythesnowflake.com

ISBN: 978-0-9795260-0-8

Library of Congress Control Number: 2007924829

Printed in the United States of America

11-11-07

For the child in all of us.

To Juanita & Lee,
I enjoyed sharing the
Book with you two!
Enjoy the great adventure
of Life! Have a great
Literary Journey!
[illegible]

CONTENTS

ACKNOWLEDGMENTS

I would like to express my sincere gratitude to my friends and colleagues who encouraged and supported me in the writing of this book:

- To my editor, Jodi Rogers, thank you for your help, your imagination, your vast vocabulary, and believing in Sammy even during those times when I did not.

- To Michelle Moser, thank you for your unwavering support and gifts along my journey.

- To Jenna and Bruce, thank you for your friendship, love, kindness, and support.

- To Jason, words can't really express my gratitude for everything you have been to me and done. Thanks dear one. The journey continues . . .

- To my various teachers, healers, and guides along the way, thank you for all of the lessons and healings.

- To my former families, thanks for the experiences and the teachings. They shaped me into who I am today.

- To my vast family, I love you all.

- To Sammy, thanks for coming into my life.

Nature is full of genius
Full of the divinity;
So that not a snowflake escapes
Its fashioning hand.

Henry David Thoreau

CHAPTER 1
The Secret Plan

Sammy was a normal snowflake. He liked his life so far in the clouds—going to snowflake school, having snowflake friends. He was an only snowflake, no brothers or sisters in his family. His parents were normal snowflake parents. His father, Nigel, worked as a college professor, and his mother, Betty, worked part-time teaching ice sculpture. His best friend, Sylvie, loved adventure and they were always getting into some kind of mischief.

One day, Sammy came home from playing and heard his parents' voices in the next room. Obviously, they hadn't heard him.

"Well, I truly feel that he is getting to the age to be told of the snowflake facts of life, Betty," said his father.

"I know, dear," replied his mother, "but he is so young and so enjoying his life. Couldn't we wait just a little bit longer? There is such innocence, such freedom, in not knowing about the true life of a snowflake and what we really go through. Do you really think he's old enough to handle all of the information?"

"Betty, I was younger than he is now when I was told," his father responded. "And thank goodness my parents chose that time, because it wasn't long afterward that I Fell with them into the Unknown. It's time, Betty. It's time."

Betty nodded in agreement. Her only child was growing up, and he needed to know what life had in store for him.

Sammy was on the stairs listening to his parents, his head reeling with questions. What did they mean by "what life had in store for him?" What was this "Falling into the Unknown"? He had heard some snowflakes at school talking about it, but he figured it was some sort of made-up story that the older flakes told in order to scare the younger ones. Could this be true?

* * * * *

Sammy sat on the steps for a long time trying to figure this out. What was he to do? He decided that, first off, he needed to find out if this were really true. He would ask his best friend, Sylvie, to see what she knew.

"Oh, you mean your parents haven't told you yet?" said Sylvie. "Mine told me 6 months ago, on my birthday. I didn't say anything because I figured you knew."

"You knew on your birthday?! And you didn't tell me?!" Snowflakes don't have yearly birthdays. They are born, and then are acknowledged by the Elders through elaborate rites of passage that honor certain qualities of maturity. Their progress through these stages depends upon how many times they have been Through the Cycle; more mature flakes have cycled innumerable times. Both Sylvie and Sammy are considered very young because they have not yet experienced the Cycle even once. "Actually, my parents haven't told me. I overheard them discussing it and deciding when they were going to tell me. So, all that they were saying is *true?*"

"As far as I know," said Sylvie. "I mean, this has been going on for as long as recorded snowflake history, and probably even before that."

Sammy became depressed. His whole world started to cave in. Everything he had ever known—everything—was going to change. And Sammy wasn't one to like change. He liked things the way they were. He liked his home, his parents, his school, his friends. He loved his life, and he sure as heck didn't want it to change.

* * * * *

It all got confirmed that night when his parents sat him down after dinner to have the Talk. They told him of the Fall into the Unknown, usually propelled by Wind (whatever that was). They said snowflakes often fell together in a group (perhaps they thought that would be comforting to hear), but sometimes it didn't happen the way they planned due to Weather. What was Weather? In fact, both his parents kept mentioning that word. All Sammy could grasp was that it was something that changed a lot, and it directly affected his status as a snowflake. He decided he didn't like Weather.

His parents went on to say that Sammy would remain intact as a snowflake until the Weather (there it was again) warmed up. Then, he would change and melt into something called water. His beautiful, frozen, crystalline body would be no longer. He would remain as this watery substance until Weather caused him to change again into vapor—invisible, no less!

"Oh, no!" Sammy thought. "This is getting worse by the minute." He will become invisible, no one will see him, and he won't be able to see anyone else. This was too much information to handle. As his mind seemed bursting with all these new concepts, he remotely heard his parents say something about the Cycle ending, yet beginning again with him changing into yet another snowflake.

"I don't understand," said a very confused Sammy. "What is melting? What is change? Am I going to die?!"

"No, no, Sammy. You are not dying," his father consoled him. "You are simply going through a metamorphosis that we all go through. Look, your mother and I have gone through this dozens of times, and we're still here. We haven't died."

Sammy excused himself and went to his room. It seemed that this thing called Weather was the culprit of all his woes. Maybe if he could change fickle Weather's mind, maybe if it could stop changing and remain the same, then he could remain the same. The trick was how to find Weather? He thought about this and decided that the only flakes who would know would be the Great and Wise Snowflake Elders at the Hidden Crystalline Monastery. Folklore states that the Monastery appears and disappears according to need. Those with heartfelt intention will have an audience with the Elders who know All There Is, Was, and Will Be. Sammy decided he would journey there and ask them where this moody Weather character lives so he may have a talk with it.

* * * * *

The next day at school, during falling lessons, he told Sylvie of his plan. (Although many of them are still not aware of the facts of snowflake life, young snowflakes are taught the skill of how to fall gracefully in preparation for their inevitable journey into the Unknown.) She nodded to him, understanding his predicament. Her turn was next. She gleefully leapt off the platform into a full swan dive, landing perfectly upright on her feet.

She looked up at her friend still on the platform and said, "Come on, Sammy. It's your turn. Just close your eyes and leap!"

"Easy for you to say," Sammy retorted. He didn't like falling, floating, diving—in other words anything having to do with being out of contact with the cloud. He liked having both feet planted. He started getting that queasy feeling in his stomach, started feeling woozy.

"Come on, Sammy. You're holding up the line!" shouted his teacher, Mrs. Tumbledown.

Sammy closed his eyes, sucked in a big breath, and leapt. He felt himself floating at first, nothing too fast. Then, he began picking up speed. Faster and faster he fell toward the ground—face first!

"Uh-oh!" Sammy thought. "I must get myself turned around before I hit the ground with my head!"

Sammy scrambled in midair, contorting his body into all kinds of positions until finally, just as he was about to make contact with the cloud, he righted himself and touched down with a loud *thump.* Although he at least landed on his feet, smooth he wasn't. Nor did he use his arms to slow his pace down to a more manageable speed.

"Goodness Sammy, are you alright?" said Mrs. Tumbledown. "Advanced trick free-falling isn't taught for another couple of years. Where did you learn that? Gracious me, you could have hurt yourself. Whatever possessed you to try that?"

At this point, all the young flakes were gathered around Sammy, congratulating him on such a cool fall.

"Wow, Sammy, that was great!"

"Awesome! I've got to try that!"

Amid all the chatter, Sammy managed to hear Sylvie's voice saying, "I can't believe you just did that. That took such courage. I would have never thought that you, of all flakes, would try a stunt like that."

Mrs. Tumbledown lifted Sammy and inspected him for any bruises or breaks. He seemed to be fine, although she suggested he go to the school nurse just in case. Sylvie said that she would accompany him to the infirmary. As the two walked together, Sylvie offered to join Sammy on his journey to visit the Elders.

"I would come along for moral support," she said. "Really, I have no beef with Weather, but I think the adventure of trekking to the Hidden Crystalline Monastery would be sensational."

Sammy felt torn. On one hand, he felt that this was his own journey to find out some answers from that temperamental Weather. On the other hand, it would be nice to have a friend along. Besides, she was better at directions than he was. Could he have his own journey, his own insights and awarenesses, and at the same time, be accompanied by a friend? Could he share his experience with Sylvie? Knowing Sylvie as a loyal and supportive companion since they were baby flakes, Sammy decided that he could. Sylvie was excited, and her enthusiasm infected him.

"Hey," he said, "I feel fine. Let's not go to the nurse. Let's go to our homes and pack for the trip to the Monastery."

"Sounds great," she replied. "Meet you in one hour at the ice sculpture in the middle of town."

CHAPTER 2
Auntie Pearl's Wisdom

The two comrades went their separate ways, excited about their upcoming adventure. It was quite easy for each of them to pack for the trip: fresh-pressed mulled apple cider, a sweater, jacket, hat, sleeping bag, tent—not much else, really. They met in the center of town, each with a backpack full of supplies. After double-checking their packs, however, they realized that they were missing the primary snowflake staple: cookies. Their favorite was Winter Flake Melts, and neither household had any extra for them to bring on the trip. Where were they going to get cookies? As they looked around in all directions, they also discovered another dilemma: which way to head—North, South, East, or West?

"I remember my mom telling me about the Elders at the Monastery," said Sylvie. "I believe she said they live on the other side of the cloud."

"Yeah, but we live in the middle, so which way is the other side?" Sammy asked.

They both pondered these first obstacles, grappling with where to stock up on their nourishment and which way to go. They decided to visit Auntie Pearl. She might know how to overcome both their obstacles. Auntie Pearl wasn't actually their aunt. She was an old snowflake who had been through the Cycle countless times and who told the most wonderful tales to all the young snowflakes. Plus, she always had the best cookies—super gooey Melts topped with an extra layer of coconut flakes!

Auntie Pearl greeted them with a plateful and invited the two travelers into her cozy igloo. She listened to their plans, let out a big sigh, pushed her glasses up on her nose, then spoke.

"This is quite an undertaking, especially for such young snowflakes," she advised. "I myself have never attempted such a journey, so I can only tell you of folklore and tales." She then closed her eyes in deep concentration. "I do know that Grandfather Sun rises in the East in the morning, replacing Grandmother Moon's night shift in their ever-present protective watch over us. Grandfather gently nudges us awake to greet the day. And by all of what I have gathered, the Great and Wise Snowflake Elders are the first flakes to greet the day. The Monastery must be in the East."

Auntie Pearl opened her eyes with both Sammy and Sylvie riveted by her words. This made logical sense to them. East is where they would head. They squirreled away as many cookies as they could fit into their packs and turned to leave, giving thanks to Auntie Pearl.

"Do your parents know of this impending trip?" the village matriarch then asked.

Sammy shot a worried glance to Sylvie. "Oh, yes," he fibbed. "Um, they are very excited about it. In fact, we are, uh, going to write a report about it for school, aren't we, Sylvie?"

"Right!" blurted Sylvie. "It's a school project. Okayed by our teacher and everything!"

Auntie Pearl nodded and bade the two farewell as they left her igloo. She wasn't totally convinced, though. She needed to do a bit of investigation herself.

* * * * *

Safely out of earshot, Sammy and Sylvie breathed a huge sigh of relief.

"We nearly blew it there," said Sammy.

"Yeah, but I think she bought our story. Besides, if she hadn't, she would have never allowed us to leave. Onward to the East!" exclaimed Sylvie.

Watching Sammy and Sylvie out of her window, Auntie Pearl was quite concerned. She decided to call their parents to alert them to their youngsters' plans. The parents thanked her and decided to have a meeting between the four of them.

Sammy's father, Nigel, felt that the children should be allowed to explore, to go on an adventure or two. "I was just as inquisitive at their age," he said. "Let them find out what the world is about by exploring it on their own a bit. It's much more vivid that way than to have us explain it to them secondhand."

Betty, Sammy's mother, seemed more hesitant. "I don't know, Nigel. They are so young, and to allow them to wander off like this . . ."

"Nigel is right, Betty," interjected Pierre, Sylvie's father. "We'll alert relatives along the way to keep an eye out for them. We'll ask the Snow Angels to keep a vigil and surround them with white light for protection. They'll be fine."

"This all sounds so optimistic," said Miriam, Sylvie's mother, "but, er, what about . . . Frostbite?" She paused and tried to swallow, the words catching in her throat.

They all shuddered, thinking of the cruel Frostbite who had brutally ransacked a whole snowflake village and killed every last flake there, even the children and pets. No one had ever exactly seen this abominable creature, yet legend had it that it existed in the Haunted Valley of the Ice Creatures and that it was fierce and ate snowflakes as a delicacy. Everyone's minds were racing with gory images of Frostbite's atrocities and how they might be wreaked on their children.

Nigel was the first to shake the trance of the creature's legend. "No snowflake in village history has ever gotten that far, not even our greatest explorers," he said. "They'll be fine. When they run out of Auntie Pearl's cookies, they'll scamper right home."

"I agree with Nigel," said Pierre. "We'll keep in touch with one another in case someone receives news. Everything will be fine, ladies."

The two mothers glanced at each other with deep concern, their intuition telling them differently than what their husbands said. However, they decided to allow their children this adventure. It was time to let go a little and let their babies explore.

* * * * *

On their way out of town, Sammy and Sylvie were accosted by Lionel, a much younger snowflake. Lionel thinks Sammy is the coolest snowflake around and that Sylvie is so pretty.

"Where are you going?" he asked.

"Oh, um, just a short hike out of town," said Sammy.

"Can I go along?" Lionel asked. "I'm big enough for a hike. Gee, it sounds like fun. You are going *out of town?*"

"Uh, no, you can't come along," said Sylvie. "This is for school, and only middle school flakes can do what we are about to do." Making this story up as she went along, she fretfully looked at Sammy for help.

"Yeah, that's right," Sammy added. "It's a school project, and we have received special permission to go outside the boundaries of the village to do it."

Sensing that they weren't telling all of the truth, Lionel said, "Well, what exactly are you doing? Can't I ask special permission, too? I'm almost a middle school snowflake. That's what I'll do! I'm going to the principal's office right now to ask *special permission.*"

Realizing that this would foil all of their plans, Sammy and Sylvie immediately stopped Lionel and told them what they were really up to. Sammy told him about the excursion to the Monastery and why they were going. Then, they made Lionel swear he wouldn't tell a soul.

"It's very important that you don't tell anyone, Lionel," said Sylvie. "This pilgrimage is for the betterment of all snowflakekind. You understand this, right?"

Sammy looked at her, amazed. He never thought that she believed that strongly in his quest. He had figured she was just going along for the ride.

Lionel nodded solemnly, understanding the enormity of their undertaking. Sammy and Sylvie thanked him for his support, promised him that he would be the first to hear of their adventure via telepathic snowflake code, gave him a cookie from each of their backpacks, and bade him good-bye.

CHAPTER 3
Big Questions

Sammy and Sylvie made their way out of town, going further than they ever had in their lives. On the outskirts of town, the vast steppes of the Central Cloud began. Further out was a rise to a huge cloud mountain.

"How are we ever going to climb this?" asked Sammy. "Maybe there is another way to go East."

"No, this is the most direct route," said Sylvie. "Besides, mountains are fun."

"Fun?" questioned Sammy, looking up skeptically.

"Yes, fun. It's a blast sliding down the other side!" Sylvie exclaimed.

Sammy wasn't too sure about this option, but he followed Sylvie, remembering that she was better at directions than he.

The cloud mountain proved higher than they both had imagined. After a couple of hours of scaling the cloud, they stopped to have a snack and rest. The rest turned into quite a nap indeed, and when they awoke, it was close to sunset. They decided to set up camp where they were. They quickly pitched their tents, smoothed their sleeping bags, and unpacked some cookies and cider to nourish them as they sat contemplating the view. After a few minutes of eating in silence and watching the vivid colors constantly shift as the West slowly absorbed the sun, Sammy spoke.

"Do you know where we come from? I mean, I know we come from our parents and all that, but I mean originally. Do you know?"

Sylvie thought for a moment and said, "I'm not sure, Sammy. Are you talking about how we first got here? You mean our ancestors, the very first snowflakes? Wouldn't that have to do with the Great Snowflake, that life force that permeates and interconnects everything? Aren't we all connected to the Great Snowflake?"

"Yeah, that's what we're told. The energy that flows through us is one and the same as the Great Snowflake. But if that is true, why do we hurt? Does the Great Snowflake hurt? If the Great Snowflake doesn't hurt, why do we have to hurt?" Sammy pondered.

"What do you mean by 'hurt'?" asked Sylvie.

"Well, I would be very hurt if my life changed and I got separated from my family and friends and my home," Sammy replied. "That's why I need to find Weather. There is some connection between Weather, change, and my happiness."

"Do you think there is some connection between the Great Snowflake and Weather?" Sylvie inquired.

"I don't know. Maybe. Maybe Weather controls the Great Snowflake, because certainly the Great Snowflake wouldn't want us to hurt . . ." Sammy paused with a look of fright. "You know, Weather might even be holding the Great Snowflake captive!" Sammy's mind was now racing. "Wow! Do you think it could be true? Oh no, that would be evil! We have to save the Great Snowflake from the grips of Evil Weather! Now we have even more reason to visit the Great and Wise Snowflake Elders at the Hidden Crystalline Monastery!"

With their minds reeling from this thought, Sammy and Sylvie retired to their separate tents and settled down to sleep in their bags. As Sammy lay there, he was more and more convinced that Weather was the culprit of all his woes and that it actually had the Great Snowflake in prison somewhere.

He soon fell asleep and dreamt of rescuing the Great Snowflake. Evil Weather, cloaked in a shroud of darkness, tried to stop them from escaping. The Great Snowflake, having regained full power since its escape from Weather's spell, simply turned around and raised one palm in Weather's direction. The mean tyrant stopped in its tracks, looking very dazed, and immediately keeled over. Sammy and the Great Snowflake continued to run outside, where they were engulfed by a cheering crowd. Sammy was a hero for rescuing the Great Snowflake. Life would return to what it once was—an unchanging course, straight and true.

* * * * *

Sammy and Sylvie awoke the next morning to a clear, crisp day. They packed up their belongings, dined on some cookies and cider, and resumed the climb up the cloud mountain. By midday, they finally reached the top to discover a spectacular view in all directions.

"Look! Over there!" exclaimed Sylvie. "That's our village!"

Sammy looked to the West, and far off into the horizon, he saw his home nestled among a group of cloud hills. Both fell silent as an ache of homesickness began to emerge inside them.

Sammy interrupted the lull. "We need to get going, to go on for the good of all snowflakes," he said.

Sylvie nodded, and they turned again to the East. In the faint distance, they could barely make out the glistening spirals of the Hidden Crystalline Monastery.

"Oh, my," said Sylvie. "There's the Monastery! Auntie Pearl was right! We are going in the right direction!" Her heart sang at the sight, knowing it was a sign that she and her companion were indeed ready to receive its gifts.

"Wow!" Sammy replied in awe, also feeling deeply honored. But fearful thoughts quickly clouded his mind. "The only thing is that the Haunted Valley of the Ice Creatures is between us and the Monastery, and I'm not looking forward to going through there."

They both shuddered at the thought of possibly seeing one of the horrific creatures from a distance or, worse yet, encountering one up close! They said a prayer for the Snow Angels to watch over them and began their descent. Sylvie, always one for speed and adventure, chose to slide down the face of the cloud mountain, squealing with joy and giggling the whole way. Sammy, on the other hand, picked his way down slowly, walking awkwardly sideways rather than smoothly sliding. Needless to say, Sylvie had to wait a full hour for him at the mountain's base.

"Well, it's about time," she said. "I was getting worried about you. Why didn't you slide? It's the most natural thing for us snowflakes to do."

"Not for this snowflake," said Sammy. Sylvie rolled her eyes at him. "Hey, I'm thirsty and hungry," remarked Sammy.

Sylvie smiled and said, "I thought you'd never bring it up! I was waiting this whole time just to share our afternoon snack together."

They both laughed as they opened their respective packs. They each pulled out a cookie and some cider and had a seat on the cloud.

Sammy looked out at the vast expanse of cloud, realizing it was such a contrast to his home. He shared his thoughts with Sylvie.

"Sylvie, this is so different from our side of the cloud mountain. Did you ever think it would look like this? I mean, I don't see any other flakes, villages, nothing here except cloudscape."

Sylvie gazed around her and took her time to answer. "You're right, Sammy. There really isn't much here on the other side of the cloud. I don't know what I was expecting. I guess maybe to meet other flakes or maybe walk through other villages, see how other flakes live." She thought a bit more. "Yeah, this looks pretty desolate and kind of dull, huh?"

Sammy looked around at his surroundings as he bit thoughtfully into his cookie. "Well, Sylvie, we're taught to appreciate everything and to see beauty everywhere, even when it is hard to." He took another contemplative bite. "Can we see the beauty in this cloudscape and appreciate it?"

Sylvie looked around. "I understand what you are saying, Sammy. I don't know, though. I am accustomed to my village, so I was comparing this cloudscape to that beauty, which is up to this point all I know."

"It's what we all do, Sylvie," replied Sammy. Sammy stood as he continued his thought. "What I am wondering is are we supposed to change our thoughts? Or change our way of seeing the world?"

"Hmmmm, I don't know Sammy," responded Sylvie. "Maybe it's not about changing our views. Maybe it's about allowing other views to be considered."

Sammy thought for a bit, "Okay, so if we allow and respect views other than our own . . . "

"Then I think we are more open to other perspectives," added Sylvie.

"Yeah, and then we can be open to whatever life brings our way," replied Sammy.

"And, and, then we are able to see the beauty in the moment, not comparing it to any other experience," exclaimed Sylvie. "Oh wow, this so sounds like transcloud travelers!"

Sammy turned and looked at his friend. At the same time, they both burst out laughing so hard that Sammy fell to the cloud where they hooted and howled for quite some time. They soon finished their snack and stood to continue their journey. At the same time, they both looked out into the horizon and saw the most beautiful rainbow. Sammy and Sylvie both took in the beauty and turned, smiling at one another. They picked up their packs and trekked into the early evening. They set up camp and had a long, restful sleep.

CHAPTER 4
Trees, Cars, Planes and People

Sammy and Sylvie woke up the next morning and continued to head East, following the gentle glow of the sunrise. About an hour into their journey, they began to hear a strange noise. It began as a faint rumbling, but soon it became louder and louder until it was a deafening throng that overwhelmed their eardrums. They realized it was coming from below their cloud and at a very high rate of speed, RIGHT TOWARDS THEM!

They ran to the nearest fog patch to hide. Just then, a huge silver bird—the biggest either had ever seen in their lives—burst through the cloud from below and continued heading upwards. They both covered their ears and, at the same time, looked in awe at this great creature soaring past them.

After the bird flew away, they emerged from their hiding place and again turned East. Suddenly, they stopped in their tracks, for there was a gaping hole in the cloud where the bird had passed through. This was definitely a snag in their plans. Sammy had been shaken enough by the thundering beast. Now, he was completely perplexed with how to get to the other side of the crater it had left behind.

"Well," Sylvie said, "we've had only a few falling lessons. We aren't supposed to start flying until next year. But isn't flying sort of like falling?"

Sammy shivered. "Oh, great," he thought, "now she's thinking of flying to the other side. I can barely fall, and she wants to fly."

Sylvie continued, "We're supposed to be able to fly innately. It's in our original crystalline makeup. My vote is to fly to the other side."

"Now wait a second here! Hold on just one slushin' snowflake second!" Sammy exclaimed. He was getting agitated with her fearlessness and her complete trust in universal nature. Did she just accept everything she was told without question? Didn't she have a mind of her own? Didn't she need to make up her own concepts? "Perhaps, just perhaps, the cloud will reshape itself and the hole will be filled." Looking at the bottomless canyon in the cloud, he really didn't believe that could happen.

Sylvie replied, "But that could take days. And we don't know what shape it will take. The hole could become bigger, or worse yet, split apart, widening this gap."

Sammy knew she was right. He hated that she was right because it meant that he had to try something new, and he had to trust that he could do that.

"Come on, Sammy, let's fly! All snowflakes can fly. We just have to believe that we can do it, and we will," Sylvie affirmed with conviction, looking him squarely in the eyes.

Sammy knew that she made sense, but he didn't like trying new things without thinking them through completely. He needed to ponder all of the possibilities from all different angles in order to make up his mind. Sylvie was asking him to decide quickly, much too quickly for his comfort. But he also knew that if he were ever to reach the Monastery before their cookie stash ran out, he needed to get going. He needed to take a leap of faith and fly.

Sammy nodded silently in agreement. Sylvie turned to the East, the wide crevasse before her. She closed her eyes and saw herself leaping into the air and soaring high over the gap to land safely on the other side. She called upon her Snow Angels for assistance. She opened her eyes, took a deep breath, and ran. She ran as fast as she could. When she reached the gap, she bravely leapt into the air without hesitating. At first she began to fall. Then, to her pleasant surprise, the downward spiral stabilized and she found herself flying! Effortlessly flying, catching the air pockets and thermals along the way.

"Weee!" she called out. "This is fun! Come on, Sammy. It's a piece of cake!"

Sammy gritted his teeth, backed up a few paces, and then ran as fast as he could toward the edge of the gap. That edge came nearer and nearer. He was almost upon it. The last thing he remembered was his footing beginning to slide. He leapt up into the air, eyes tightly shut, arms waving madly, legs kicking in opposite directions.

"Open your eyes, Sammy!" Sylvie yelled excitedly. "It's a glorious flight!"

Sammy took a deep breath and slowly peeked through one wincing eye. He looked around. He opened the other eye, taking in the whole scene. Sylvie was right. It *is* glorious, if not downright fun, to fly.

"Sammy, be aware of your direction!" Sylvie shouted. "Remember how to turn. Turn, Sammy, turn!"

Sammy was so enthralled with the scenery that he forgot all about navigation. He was headed straight for a collision with a cloud cliff! He scrambled in the air, arms and legs flailing to change his course. Graceful he was not, but he managed to land safely next to Sylvie on the other side of the canyon.

"Whew! That was a close one, Sylvie. Thanks for looking out for me," Sammy said. Sylvie nodded and smiled, inspired by her friend's courage. They looked around, found East, and continued on their journey.

* * * * *

The rest of the trek that day proved to be an easy stroll. The two friends decided to break early and set up camp underneath a protective cloud overhang. They lay on their backs and watched the other clouds roll by. They played the familiar cloud game, "Find the Shape."

"There's a dragon!" exclaimed Sylvie.

"Oh, there's Professor Flake with his big ears and glasses!" said Sammy. They both giggled.

"I see a smokestack over there," Sylvie said, pointing in another direction.

"What's a smokestack?" Sammy asked.

"Well, it looks like that cloud over there," she replied. "I mean, I have only seen pictures of one, but when we Fall into the Unknown, some of us might land on one. Once I heard how those things might actually make us Fall into the Unknown faster, and maybe not return."

"Not return?!" Sammy cried, completely alarmed at this news. "Whad'ya mean, 'not return'?"

"Well . . . when my older sister was going through her first Rite of Passage, I *just happened* to overhear the Elder give this teaching to her."

"Sylvie!" exclaimed a shocked Sammy, "Rites of Passage Ceremonies are private. How did you '*just happen* to overhear' their conversation?"

"Oh, I *just happened* to be sitting within earshot on the stairs, the door was opened, and— "

"You spied on your sister's Rite of Passage Ceremony?" gasped an incredulous Sammy.

"Uh, wel-l-l, uh, yes, I guess that's what I did," stammered Sylvie with downcast eyes. "I was walking down the stairs to go out, the door was slightly opened, and the words were so intriguing that I just had to stop and listen."

This admission seemed to pacify Sammy. It was not an intentional, premeditated spying, but a chance occurrence that gave Sylvie vast insight into Falling into the Unknown. He decided to forgive her trespass and nodded for her to continue.

"Anyway, somehow those things and other machines called cars cause what's called global warming. And forest destruction is making it worse."

"What's a forest?" inquired Sammy.

"Trees, silly. A bunch of trees," Sylvie gently chided him. "Trees are able to store a large amount of what's called car bone mon ox ice, car bone mon ox, mon ox . . . Oh, dear, I can't remember, but I know it's one of the major gases that creates global warming, and the trees help remove it from the air. So, if there are fewer trees, then there is more of that gas. You know what a car is?"

Sammy nodded. He'd seen a picture of one in the *Flakedom Daily News.* She continued, "Well, cars emit that gas also. More cars, less trees, more people . . ."

"People?" Sammy questioned.

"People. The highest form of intelligence on Earth," Sylvie said matter of factly. "Anyway, all of these factors are making everything so hot that Weather becomes unstable, which interrupts our Cycle."

Sammy thought for a few moments, absorbing all of this. Finally he said quietly, "Sylvie, who's in charge of the cars?"

"The people," she replied.

"And the smokestacks?" he questioned.

"The people," she said, not quite knowing where he was going with this line of thought.

"Who is eliminating the trees?" he went on.

"The people, Sammy, the people," Sylvie cried, finally grasping what Sammy was piecing together.

"Well, I don't understand. If they are so intelligent, why are they destroying the planet and atmosphere, causing harm to everything, including us? Do they know what they're doing? Surely if they are the highest form of intelligence, they wouldn't do something to harm others on purpose, right? I mean, that would be cruel," Sammy said, his mind exploding with all these new concepts.

"I think it's illogical behavior, Sammy. It doesn't make sense to me," Sylvie said, shaking her head.

There was silence between the two as they both allowed their conversation to settle in. After awhile, Sylvie broke the heaviness.

"The Elder also said that if global warming continues in some areas on Earth, like this really important section called the Artic, we might Fall and not return to the clouds."

Finally, the information he was waiting for! This could seriously jeopardize his status as a snowflake. "Go on," he said stoically.

"The mystics believe that with all of the warming of the atmosphere, it could be a prelude to an Ice Age, because the last Ice Age occurred when the Earth was warming, only this time it's warming much faster due to the people," replied Sylvie.

"Whoa, Ice Age? Well, wouldn't that be good for us flakes?" Sammy reasoned.

"Not necessarily," continued Sylvie. "The Shaman Elder went on to say that with the Artic regions warming, more water would evaporate in the summer and fall onto land as snow in the winter."

"That sounds okay," interrupted Sammy.

"And due to unstable Weather caused by the gases, all of the snow might not melt again in the spring, and then glaciers would form," she said.

"Yeah, and . . ."

"And we could end up in an Ice Age, stuck on a glacier, and never see our beautiful cloud homes again," Sylvie said with finality.

"Never see our cloud homes again?" Sammy meekly uttered.

Sylvie shook her head. Sammy shuddered with this new input about Falling into the Unknown. There could be a reason for Weather's unpredictability. Just the thought of it made his conviction that much stronger to reach the

Monastery in order to receive the knowledge of Weather's whereabouts. He would find Weather, and once and for all, extract the truth about its volatile nature. He would do this for the good of all snowflakekind. His courageous resolve was interrupted by another shape.

"I see a two-headed monster over there!" he shouted.

Sylvie looked up where Sammy was pointing to the cloud: it was huge, with two vicious faces and fire coming out of both of its mouths. They both shivered at the same time. They knew they were close to the Haunted Valley of the Ice Creatures and hoped that Frostbite didn't look like that monstrous cloud. In fact, they hoped they would skirt through the Valley with no encounter with any monsters at all.

Breaking the ominous silence, Sylvie spotted another shape. "That one over there looks like your dog, Crystal," she said.

Sammy looked in the direction where Sylvie was pointing. Just hearing Crystal's name made him feel homesick. Seeing her shape in the cloud was almost more than he could stand. He watched that cloud for a long time, thinking of his home, family, and friends. He fell asleep believing that he was going to make things right for all, not just for himself. And that felt like a good thing.

CHAPTER 5
Descent into Darkness

The next morning, Sylvie and Sammy noticed they were even nearer to the Haunted Valley of the Ice Creatures than they had realized the night before. An ominous silence pervaded as they neared the Valley. The joy from the day seemed to evaporate as their hearts began to quicken. There was a foreboding chill in the air; the temperature was actually dropping as they walked toward the Valley. Both of the adventurers shivered. They stopped, took a deep breath, and decided they needed a plan for crossing that eerie expanse.

"Well," said Sammy, "I figure that since we flew over that gap made by the airplane, maybe we can fly over the Valley." He had finally solved the mystery of the silver beast that ripped that crater through their cloud. It had way too many eyes for a bird, and it didn't seem to have a beak.

Little did they know that the Valley was huge—miles wide. They arrived at its edge and looked down. It looked miles deep, too. They were just small little snowflakes. There was no way they could fly to the other side. What were they to do? The only plan they could fathom was to walk into the Valley to reach the other side. But then, they would certainly meet Frostbite. What to do, they wondered.

"Well, Auntie Pearl said that Frostbite sleeps during the day and hunts at night," Sylvie remembered. "So, if we walk now until dark and then hide, we should be okay" She then hesitated, "Or was it that he slept during the night and hunted during the day? Oh, dear, I believe that I've forgotten. Oh, no, what are we going to do?"

Sammy sat down to ponder the question. He was good at pondering. He liked taking his time to make decisions. He needed a cookie, though, to help him to think clearly. Sylvie handed him one as he thought. Flying was not an option. He looked for a bridge; none in sight. The problem was that no other snowflakes in their village had ever gotten this far. But he had a purpose, an intention. He had to get to the other side of the Valley and onward to the Monastery to ask his question of the Elders. Although he was scared, he knew that the only way for them right now was to walk down into the Valley and up the other side.

"We walk, Sylvie," he said with grim resolve. "We walk."

For the first time in her life, Sylvie was scared. But she also felt Sammy's courage. She wasn't sure where he found such strength, but it felt comforting to have him be the bold one. It seemed to quell her fears enough that she could quietly say, "Okay, let's go."

They picked up their backpacks, and, already well into the fourth day of their journey, they headed directly into the Haunted Valley of the Ice Creatures. As the late morning shifted into afternoon, they climbed deeper into the Valley. The deeper they hiked, the darker and scarier the place became.

They were completely surrounded by strange, towering ice shapes, which were twisted and contorted in bizarre positions, making it very difficult to find their direction. The ice was so dense and layered that light could not pass through it clearly and instead, fell onto the ground in creepy, long shadows. Sammy and Sylvie, wide-eyed and barely breathing, took slow, cautious steps. Acutely aware of any strange sounds, they picked their way through the menacing ice forest. They wanted to get through it quickly, yet it was so hard to find their way. "What were these strange shapes? Why were they there, at the beginning of the Valley? Were they warnings to adventurers to turn back?" the young snowflakes wondered.

In her effort to gingerly pass these strange carvings, Sylvie accidentally bumped into one of the sculptures. All of a sudden, a long, piercing wail emanated from the interior of the ice! Sylvie screamed, jumped in the air, and landed a full 30 feet away! Having her wits scared out of her, she found herself strewn flat on her back in complete terror and bewilderment.

A protective Sammy made sure she was okay, and then walked cautiously over to the "sculpture." Upon closer observation, he found himself looking into the lifeless eyes of an oddly shaped snowflake, seemingly trapped inside a frozen prison. It stared back at him with a vapid gaze, opened its black hole of a mouth, and let out another crystal-shattering shriek. The force of the cry hit Sammy hard, going right through him and throwing him on the ground. He sprang up, backed away, grabbed Sylvie's hand, and the two of them ran down a path. They kept running until they needed to catch their breath.

"What was that, Sammy?" asked Sylvie, as she gulped for air.

"I-I-I don't know," said a befuddled Sammy. "It looked like some kind of snowflake that got mangled up pretty badly."

"Does this mean that all these ice sculptures contain monsters?" cried Sylvie.

"I-I-I don't know, Sylvie," he replied fretfully. "I don't know why they are trapped in there. Who put them there? Why can't they escape? Do they want to escape? Oh no! Maybe they are food for Frostbite!"

They both shuddered at such a thought. Sammy knew they had to get through the Valley of the Ice Creatures quickly, even more so now. As they continued, the ice forest was becoming thicker and dimmer, making it more difficult to see ahead and keep direction. Chaotic brambles of ice branches, sharp as swords, seemed to jut out in every direction, making their already-tentative path treacherous. The eerie chorus of anguish from the prisoners haunted them from a distance, while the raw Wind hissed all around them.

"Are we still going East?" asked Sammy.

Sylvie looked around to find the sun, but the surroundings were so dense that she couldn't see it. "I d-d-don't know, Sammy," she stammered. "I'm a little turned around, I think. I'm not sure which way is East."

They put their backpacks down to assess the situation. They were in the thick of the Valley, and being so tiny, could not see the sky. As they looked around to determine their direction, the light became dimmer, as though something was blocking it. Sammy and Sylvie looked at one another as the light was mysteriously and quickly fading, and then Sylvie remembered the whispered warnings from the villagers about the dangers of the Valley. There was only one thing they knew that was big enough to block the sun. Frostbite! They turned slowly at the same time and looked behind them. There he was: the most notorious snowflake monster of all time, and they were face to face with him!

As he bared his rows of barbed fangs, Sammy had a flash of the story about how Frostbite unmercifully killed a whole village—men, women, children, animals, even baby snowflakes and their tiny snowflake kittens—by rolling down a snowy cloud mountain in order to gain speed and mass. He timed this premeditated massacre when most would be home relaxing after dinner. He hit the village hard and fast, taking all by surprise. His giant form steamrolled through the town, flattening everything in its path. There were no survivors. The only remains of that fateful day were the mangled snowflake bodies and debris from destroyed family igloos. They say Frostbite was knocked unconscious by the horrific spree. The story goes that when he came to, he looked around, bared his teeth, pounded his chest and emitted a great howl as if he were proud of what he had done. After that, he ran away, never to be seen again.

Sammy and Sylvie screamed, turned in midair, and started scrambling for their lives, running as fast as they could. Sammy wished he had been old enough for flying class; his little legs did not seem to be going fast enough. He looked back once and saw the vicious beast striding in his direction with his mouth open, licking his serrated chops.

"Oh, no!" Sammy thought. "Where are we going to hide from this brute?" Luckily, they were so much smaller and quicker than he that they were able to scurry into a burrow in a cloudbank and hide. Frostbite walked past the bank and stopped. He listen for sounds and, hearing none, grunted, sighed, and continued looking for his prey elsewhere.

* * * * *

Sylvie and Sammy decided to stay in the warm hideaway for a while and catch their breath. They both snuggled in and took a nap. When they awoke, it was midafternoon, and they were hungry. Where were they to find food? They had left their packs on the ground when they were frightened by Frostbite.

"Maybe we should stay here for the night," Sylvie proposed, "since we don't have our tent or sleeping bags. At least we will be protected, and in the morning, we can decide what to do."

Sammy agreed, so the two young snowflakes fell back asleep in their cozy nest. Little did they know that this was the laboratory for Dr. Cirro Thunderhead, the most renowned, yet elusive, scientist in all flakedom. He and his assistant, Nimbo, had been out for the day, collecting specimens for the doctor's research on the rapid rise of deformities amongst snowflakes.

Nimbo was an abnormal flake since birth, having no organized crystalline construction, no points, only rounded edges. He was the first irregular flake to be studied by Dr. Thunderhead. The two formed a strong bond and thus, Nimbo became his assistant, committed to finding the reason why he and so many others were born this way. The two returned to the laboratory only to find the intruders sound asleep.

"My, who do we have here?" asked Nimbo.

"I dare say, Nimbo, it looks like some young snowflakes—very far from home," replied the elderly Dr. Thunderhead, who himself was missing a few crystals.

"Wow, real, whole snowflakes!" said Nimbo. "So this is what I'm supposed to look like? Look at their points—so many of them! And, and look at the delicate, intricate designs of their torso. Oh my, see the way the light reflects off of them, sparkly, so very sparkly. I am not sparkly at all . . . They are so beautiful. I am so ugly. Doctor, what happened to me? What happened to all of those in the ice? What happened to all of us? When will this madness stop?" Nimbo began to sob, his whole body shaking from the weight of his own sadness.

The good doctor placed his arms around his friend. "Oh, my dear Nimbo," he said. "You are not ugly. You are simply different. You know that no two flakes are the same. You have your own beauty, Nimbo, your wonderful, kind heart. I have devoted all of my life's research to finding a reason why in the last 50 years, more and more flakes have been so drastically different than others. It is my promise to you and snowflakekind that I will find out why." With that gesture of compassion, Nimbo let out a long, painful cry.

All of this commotion stirred Sammy and Sylvie awake to find both Dr. Thunderhead and Nimbo peering at them about an inch from their tiny snowflake noses. One look at the monstrous Nimbo and they both screamed. This startled the good doctor and assistant, so they screamed back. Within seconds, chaos broke out, with everyone shouting, scrambling, and running in all directions. Sylvie and Sammy managed to escape with all crystals intact and ran outside into the biting air. They kept running until they reached a clearing, where they stopped to catch their breath.

"What *was* that?" Sylvie gasped.

Sammy quivered with fright. "I have no idea, but I sure didn't want to hang out there to find out!"

They looked around and realized they were next to a beautiful pond, entirely iced over and covered with delicate snow. In the moonlight, Sammy could see something lying on the ground not far from them. The objects were not moving. He slowly crept forward, being as quiet as he could until he came within a safe distance and recognized the shapes as their backpacks! Frostbite must have dropped them after he was finished with them. Most likely, there was no food left, but at least they had their tent and sleeping bags.

Sammy picked both of them up and noticed that they felt heavier. Not knowing at all what to expect at this point, he gingerly opened his pack in the metallic light. Lo and behold, there was a fresh batch of cookies, still warm, and more juice! Sylvie quickly opened her pack to discover the same—more provisions for the journey. Although they did not understand who did this (certainly not the cruel Frostbite), they were grateful for their good fortune and thanked the Great Snowflake. Since they were both awake at this hour, Sylvie and Sammy decided to eat some of the yummy cookies and continue on their way East.

* * * * *

Frostbite watched them from a distance, grinning from ear to ear upon seeing them accept his gift. He realized that his big size scared them. And, he had such a horrible reputation for being fierce, mean, and snowflake-eating. It wasn't true. However, he knew all too well how those rumors started, after the tragic accident that decimated his village. He was coming home after being away for so very long. He was looking forward to seeing his elderly parents and his grown siblings. He had run away when he was a young flake because his crystalline structure was so badly deformed. He couldn't take the nasty comments, the jeering, the heckling, and the name-calling. On his way down the cloud mountain, he tripped and fell. He began to roll down the mountain toward his village, and he couldn't stop. He had no points to stop his momentum. He screamed to warn the villagers, but no one heard him. All was lost. He immediately went into hiding after realizing that there was no one left for him to love.

Unfortunately, cloud gossip kept the rumors alive, and they left him desperately lonely. Life was hard as Frostbite, and he wanted friends to play with. He decided to follow the two young adventurers at a safe distance and maybe, just maybe, they could become friends. Maybe they would accept him.

CHAPTER 6
An Unexpected Friend

Sammy and Sylvie finished their delicious meal, packed their bags, and began walking toward the Hidden Crystalline Monastery. The sun began to rise in the East as they embarked upon the fifth day of their journey. It was a welcomed sight as they approached the Valley's deep-rutted canyon. Traveling at night was not their cup of tea, especially with Frostbite lurking about.

They really wanted to move through the canyon as swiftly as possible, but it was so dense and they were so little that it was hard to maintain direction or speed. Once in awhile, Sylvie would fly to the top of an ice formation to locate where they were, although because of what happened before, she did this with great caution. She could handle that amount of flying, however it took an extreme amount of energy and concentration to do it. She would close her eyes, focus on her breath, and envision herself flying. She dedicated all of her inner being on flying, and then, it would simply happen.

She reached the top of the formation to find their direction. It was the same one that Frostbite was hiding behind at that very moment. Sylvie looked around and located the East. "It's that way, Sammy," she said.

Sammy looked from whence they came. "It can't be. We just came from there." He looked around. "Oh, no," he thought, "we have just made a complete circle." They were right where they had started four hours ago. "We're walking in circles!" Sammy cried.

Distressed with this news, Sylvie craned her neck, looking around from her frozen perch. Suddenly, she lost her balance, and before she knew what was happening, she was falling. She didn't know how to start flying during a fall. She just could not get her wits about her or recover her breathing. She panicked and screamed to Sammy to catch her.

Sammy began running toward her. Before anyone knew what was happening, her falling stopped and she was gently placed on the ground. She stepped away, gazing curiously at Sammy, who was facing her. His eyes and mouth were wide open; he could not speak.

"What is it, Sammy?" Sylvie asked. She was wondering how she managed not to hurt herself during the fall. What saved her? "What's wrong? What's going on? Sammy, talk to me. You're scaring me!"

All Sammy could do was point. She followed his finger behind her. As she turned around, Sylvie came face-to-face with a pair of enormous, misshapen feet. Her heart began to pound as she lifted her head further and further back, taking in more and more of the view.

"Oh, my," she thought, "I know of only one thing in this world with feet this huge." Sure enough, as she tilted her head as far as it would go, there was Frostbite, staring down at them, bearing his craggy teeth.

Or was he smiling? Sylvie could have sworn the corners of his strange mouth were turned upward. In any case, a grinning Frostbite is a terrifying sight. Those rows of teeth, a menacing mess of broken glass, made Sammy and Sylvie scream.

He quickly said, "Please don't be scared of me. I have no friends because no one gives me a chance. People believe the tales about me and don't get to know the real me. Everyone just automatically runs when they see me." At this point, his eyes became a bit watery. "Please don't run away. Please stay. In fact, let me help you on your way. Where are you going? Why are you in the Valley of the Ice Creatures?"

* * * * *

At first, neither of the young snowflakes could move, much less talk. Sylvie found her voice first. "We, we are, um, on our way to see the Great and Wise Snowflake Elders at the Hidden Crystalline Monastery. Isn't that right, Sammy?"

Sammy gulped, not knowing quite what to do. But since his legs would not move, he joined the conversation. "Uh, that's right, Sylvie. Um, the problem is, we have lost our way in this Valley. It's so dense with ice and snow, and we are so small that we can't seem to maintain an easterly course."

Frostbite smiled even more broadly. Sammy and Sylvie shuddered at the sight of more teeth. The mammoth snowflake spoke, "Oh, I can help you two. Why don't you ride on my shoulders, and I would be more than happy to escort you to the other side of the canyon. From my height, I can see the Monastery from here."

This news excited Sammy and Sylvie. The Monastery was close, in view, no less! Yet, they hesitated. Could this be one of Frostbite's ploys to trap them in one of those ice prisons like all those other poor snowflakes, torturing them for weeks, even years, before he devoured their little bodies with his endless hunger? Was he really trying to help, or just trick them? Could they take the risk and trust him?

"How can we trust you, after what you did?" Sammy demanded.

"No, no, you don't understand," Frostbite said, his eyes watering again. "I didn't kill off my whole village on purpose. I would never do that to those I love! It was a horrible accident. I was returning home after being away for a long time. I wanted to see my elderly parents, brothers, and sisters. Because I am physically challenged, it's hard for me to walk. I tripped high on the cloud mountain and started to tumble down toward my village. I couldn't stop. I just couldn't stop. I don't have the points to stop." He was visibly shaking as he sobbed. "This terrible catastrophe has left me lonely and heartbroken for all of my days."

The two young snowflakes also teared up. Their hearts melted as they finally learned the truth of Frostbite's past. Looking around at their grim circumstances, Sammy and Sylvie decided Frostbite's offer was their best option after all.

Taking the risk, they introduced themselves to their new friend and discovered that Frostbite's real name was Aaron. They quickly overcame their fear of this colossus and stepped into the soft cup of his gigantic hand. He placed them delicately, one on each shoulder, and began the journey East through the Valley as their guide.

* * * * *

Aaron was right. The view was magnificent from such a height. They could see almost all the way home in one direction, and in the other, the spirals of the Hidden Crystalline Monastery grew larger and clearer with each step. Sammy and Sylvie thrilled in every cell of their body: their intention beckoned the Monastery to reveal itself after all! Aaron proved to be a cordial host in his neck of the woods. He presented different points of interest, including lovely views and descriptions of who lived where and for how long. The young snowflakes asked him about the two flakes that scared them in the hollow of the sculpture where they had first encountered him.

"Oh, that's Dr. Cirro Thunderhead and his assistant, Nimbo," Aaron said. "A flake of great compassion and genius, the doctor has dedicated his life's work to researching why there are so many deformities amongst snowflakes. It was Nimbo who probably scared you, as I initially did. We were both born this way. This Valley is a safe refuge for all of us snowflakes who are 'different' and unpleasing to the eye. It is better for us to live here than to endure the ridicule from the 'normal' flakes. At least we receive love and support from one another, which is very much needed."

Both Sammy and Sylvie fell silent. They suddenly realized how easy a life they have had so far. No pain and suffering like the flakes they have encountered in the Valley. Sammy finally broke the silence.

"Aaron, why are those flakes frozen in the ice? One frightened us terribly with its wailing and crying. I felt so awful for it, I-I didn't know what to do. But we were so scared, we ran from it."

Aaron looked away with sad eyes. "That is self-induced, my little friends," he said with great effort. "Those flakes have suffered so greatly that they would prefer not to engage in life. So, layer upon layer of protective ice built up around them until finally, they became trapped by their own frozen fears. It so saddens me to see them like that, but there really isn't anything for me to do, either."

"Nothing can free them?" both Sammy and Sylvie inquired at the same time.

"Well, I am told that if all the flakes in flakedom gathered with open, loving hearts full of kindness and compassion, that act would melt the ice and free those inside. Then, through understanding and acceptance, the ice would melt inside these wounded flakes, around their frigid hearts. They would accept themselves through the example of being accepted by society. But that is nearly an impossible task. I mean, look at the rumors about me, how they have sustained all these Cycles, with no one except you two investigating the truth around them."

Sammy felt Aaron's sorrow, and it made him sad. He had never seen "different" flakes before entering the Valley, and now, everywhere he looked, he saw them. "What had occurred to make this happen here in the clouds?" he wondered. He wanted to do something for these snowflakes, but as Aaron said, there was only one way to melt the ice. All the snowflakes had to gather, radiating loving kindness and compassion. It would be nearly impossible to assemble one village together with one intention, much less the whole cloud!

As these thoughts filtered through Sammy's mind, he brought his attention back to the present moment. He and his best friend were currently sitting on a monster's shoulder, being personally shepherded through the Haunted Valley of the Ice Creatures. Who would have thought that he and Sylvie would have become friends with Frostbite? Life was surely unpredictable. Sammy wasn't quite sure if he liked that, though. It reminded him of change, which he knew he didn't like.

But Sammy looked at his new friend and realized that he had followed other flakes' opinions about Aaron and, thus, had not formed his own ideas from direct experience. He simply heeded the common belief of his village that Frostbite was a merciless murderer with no regard for life, a heartless cannibal who massacred his own kind without warning. By overcoming his fears, Sammy discovered that Aaron was not like that at all. He was generous, funny and, in fact, a vegetarian.

Life sure was taking some strange turns for Sammy. Now he had two friends on this pilgrimage, Sylvie and Aaron, instead of only one, and all three of them were on their way to the magical Crystalline Monastery to have an audience with the Great and Wise Snowflake Elders. Life was good, so very good.

CHAPTER 7
The Destined Trio

As they made their way through the Valley of the Ice Creatures, Aaron asked, "Why are you two going to the Monastery anyway?"

"Well," said Sammy, "I want to learn how to locate Weather."

"Weather? Why?" Aaron inquired.

Sylvie piped up, "Because he doesn't like change, and it seems that snowflakes have to change according to Weather."

"Right," said Sammy. "I figure that if I can talk some sense into Weather and get it to stop changing, then I don't have to change and everything will be like it is—the same! I like being a snowflake. I like me now. I don't want to change, and I sure as heck don't want to Fall into the Unknown or any of that nonsense. I just want life to be the way it is right now."

Aaron listened attentively to Sammy, realizing that life had, indeed, changed for the young snowflake. Where once Sammy was timid, he was now courageous; where once they were frightened of one another, they were now friends. Sammy could now leap, free fall, and sort of fly; before he could not. Aaron decided not to bring up any of this right now. He enjoyed his new companions and didn't want to ruffle any crystals so early in their friendship. Besides, he had never been to the Hidden Crystalline Monastery and was curious about it.

"Would you two mind if I went all the way to the Monastery with you?" Aaron asked. "I have never been, and I, too, have some questions for the Great and Wise Elders."

"What would you like to know?" Sylvie wondered.

With a heavy sigh, Aaron looked at them with his large, sad eyes and unloaded his painful questions. "Why was I born abnormal? Why did the whole accident have to happen? Why did I have to lose everyone I loved? Why won't anyone believe that it was an accident, that I wouldn't hurt anything? Why do I have to be persecuted for something that's already painful enough for me? Why don't flakes give me a chance? Why don't they get to know me before forming an opinion about me? Why do judgments need to be formed anyway?"

Both Sammy and Sylvie gazed at their new friend, realizing they were both guilty of much that he had just described. Aaron had a tear in his eye. They could see he was upset, and it pained them.

He continued, "I don't know. Maybe I have to do something different, or be different, or change some part of myself in order to be accepted and less threatening."

Sammy and Sylvie exchanged glances and nodded. "Of course, you can come along to the Crystalline Monastery. We would be honored to have you with us," they both exclaimed, filling in each other's words to express their unified thought.

That made Aaron feel a whole lot better. He smiled at them both, one on each shoulder. The trio continued their journey East, happy to have each other for company.

As the sun began to set, they realized they were about halfway through the Valley. It was decided to stop, set up camp, and eat before dark. As Sammy and Sylvie were setting up their tents, they realized that there was no room for their large friend.

"Oh, don't worry about me," said Aaron. "I'll just gather some snow and icicles. They will make a fine bed."

Sammy and Sylvie still had some cookies and juice. They offered some to Aaron.

"Thank you, but I prefer roots and winter berries," he said as he began to forage for his dinner.

Sammy and Sylvie shrugged their shoulders, eating their cookies as Aaron found all sorts of strange food for himself. They all sat in silence, enjoying the rich violet sunset, savoring their respective meals.

Sammy's mind wandered to thoughts of his home. Both of his parents would be returning home from work. His mother would begin fixing a wonderful, warm dinner. His father would help, the two of them talking about their workdays. He could hear their voices, gentle laughter, the way they lovingly greeted him after a hard day of play. His dog,

Crystal, would be begging for food, or at least a treat. He began to feel homesick again.

He immediately shook off the feelings by reminding himself that he had a mission that could affect all snowflake life for the better. Knowing this, Sammy's mood brightened and his attention returned back to the group and the sweetly fading sun.

"Well, I think I'm going to go to sleep now," yawned Aaron. Sylvie and Sammy nodded in agreement. They each turned in and fell asleep almost immediately.

* * * * *

The sunrise was spectacular the next morning as Sammy and Sylvie awakened to the wonderful scent of hot chocolate and spiced porridge.

"Wow, Aaron, this smells great!" exclaimed a very hungry Sammy.

"Yeah, where did you get all of this food?" a salivating Sylvie chimed in while dipping a finger into the pot of chocolate.

"Oh, it's just a little something I whipped up. I hope you two like it," a humble Aaron replied, looking a bit embarrassed.

A few minutes later, all three were eating the scrumptious meal.

"This is excellent, Aaron. We name you camp chef!" proclaimed Sylvie. Sammy seconded the motion. Aaron beamed from head to toes, pleased with his new position.

"Well, now, I believe if we walk a lot today and not take too many breaks, we should arrive at the Crystalline Monastery by tomorrow afternoon," Aaron calculated.

This information thrilled Sammy and Sylvie. This is what the whole expedition was about! By tomorrow, they would be at the Monastery door, asking for entrance to see an Elder.

CHAPTER 8
The Turning Point

The trio quickly packed their belongings and headed on their way. Luckily, Weather cooperated perfectly with their plans. They didn't take too many breaks, and by early afternoon of the next day, the only thing between them and the Hidden Crystalline Monastery was the most immense field of ice. It sprawled before them like a crystal carpet. The Monastery itself sparkled in the light like millions of tiny diamonds whose prisms cast swirling rainbows of pure hue throughout the surrounding sky and snow. They had arrived! All three were elated that they had gotten this far.

Laughing and giggling with hearts pumping quickly, Aaron, Sammy, and Sylvie were congratulating one another on a journey well trekked. Suddenly, a fine mist passed over them. They inhaled the sweetest perfume they had ever smelled. And was that music they heard very faintly in the distance? Or maybe chanting?

Immediately, their hearts stopped racing and returned to a calm state. In fact, as they looked around, the whole area seemed to exude peace. Absorbing what was happening, Sammy looked at his two friends and smiled. The three friends were struck speechless by this experience and the exquisite beauty before them. They couldn't find words to explain it, but all they knew was that they felt calm, happy, and peaceful. No one knew how much time lapsed before Aaron spoke.

"Well, I guess we should march onward, although I'm not sure about my footing on this i-i-i-ice!" Aaron suddenly slipped, his feet flew up in the air, and he landed on his back, catapulting his passengers in different directions.

Sammy landed headfirst in a snow bank. He managed to pull himself out and then immediately thought of Sylvie.

"Sylvie, where are you? Are you okay? Are you hurt?" Sammy called out frantically.

Sylvie replied, "I'm okay. I'm here, Sammy. No, no, up here. Straight up. Look straight up."

Sammy followed her directions and found Sylvie high in an ice formation. Neither had any visible bumps or bruises, though, and that was a relief. After taking a few calming breaths, Sylvie fell gracefully to the ice field and joined her friends.

"Oh, my goodness, Sammy, what happened to Aaron?" she said, pointing at the huge, limp mass lying face up on the ice. "Oh, dear, what are we going to do?" she wailed. "We're just little snowflakes. How can we possibly help him?"

Sammy looked at his newfound friend. Frostbite was knocked out cold from the fall on the ice. Sammy was torn because he was so close to the Crystalline Monastery, so close to the goal of having his questions answered. But his friend Aaron needed his attention. He looked up at the glistening Monastery gently beckoning him to come forth with his questions, assuring him of answers. He looked down at Aaron, such a large beast, yet at this moment looking so helpless and not fierce at all. Almost snowflake-like.

Suddenly, a light came on inside Sammy. He wondered whether Aaron, the feared creature known as Frostbite, was just like him. As he expanded this thought, he realized there really was no difference between Aaron and himself. They were the same. They came from the same source, the Great Snowflake. Sammy knew he needed to treat Aaron the same as how he wanted to be treated.

Right there, he decided the Hidden Crystalline Monastery could wait another day or two, or whatever it took, until Aaron felt better to venture onward. He realized he couldn't leave his friend behind. He had to stay with him.

As Sammy arrived at these awarenesses, he turned his head once more toward the Monastery. But much to his chagrin, the elusive cloister was gone! It had disappeared from sight!

Yet, in the faint distance, a lone Snowflake Elder was walking toward Sammy, dressed entirely in white, glistening from head to toe. Sammy looked up and was nearly blinded by the light shining forth. He shielded his vision so he could look directly at the wise one approaching him. As the Elder drew closer, Sammy found himself looking up into the most beautiful, kindest, clearest blue eyes he had ever seen. The Elder smiled serenely, gazing back into Sammy's eyes. She broadened her smile, and Sammy felt his heart expand in all directions, as though it would pop out of his chest. She nodded at him, turned, and gracefully walked away, gradually disappearing again into the distance.

In that moment, Sammy understood. He had changed. His heart had opened, and he realized that he was okay and that change was okay. In fact, change was necessary for life's journey. Sammy felt content for the first time in his life. Content with being a snowflake. Content with knowing that change was inevitable. Content with the experience of being just as it is.

He smiled at Sylvie. She hadn't seen the Elder. She didn't need to. She understood deep inside her being that Sammy's quest had been fulfilled. She was happy for her friend, happy that he found his truth. She realized that they could go home now.

But that is another journey, another story for another time.

Sylvie's Winter Flake Melts

Sylvie's Cookies are both healthy and amazingly delicious. With crispy edges and soft, chewy centers, they are best eaten while still warm. Follow the directions with an Elder in your life, and you, too, can feast like your snowflake friends. This recipe makes about 12 to 15 cookies.

Ingredients:

1/2 cup soymilk
1/2 cup safflower oil (or any light, mild oil)
1/2 cup brown rice syrup
1/2 cup maple syrup
2 cups rolled oats (not quick-cooking)
1 cup whole wheat flour or Spelt flour
2 teaspoons baking powder
2 teaspoons ground cinnamon
1 cup or more chopped walnuts (optional)
1/2 cup or more raisins
3 ripe bananas
coconut flakes sprinkled on top, according to taste

Directions:

1) Preheat oven to 350°F. Lightly coat cookie sheet with nonstick spray or oil.

2) Stir first four ingredients together until well blended, and then mix in oats.

3) Sift flour, baking powder, and cinnamon over the wet mixture. Add walnuts and raisins. Stir until well mixed.

4) Peel bananas, mash on a plate with a fork, and add to mixture.

5) Drop large spoonfuls of batter onto the cookie sheet. Bake for about 25 minutes or until cookies are golden brown at edges.

Sammy's Hot Mulled Cider

Sammy's Cider is a sweet treat for any time of year. Serve hot in a mug with a cinnamon stick for winter warmth and cheer, or cold over ice for unique summer refreshment. Find out what gave Sammy and Sylvie nourishment, energy, and strength during their long journey across the cloud.

Ingredients:

2 quarts pressed apple cider
2 sticks cinnamon
5 whole cloves
1 whole nutmeg (optional)
1 cup honey or maple syrup

Directions:

1) Combine cider, honey/syrup, and spices in pot.

2) Mull slowly on low to medium heat. Do not allow to boil.

3) Cook to taste, for at least an hour.

SAVE THE SNOWFLAKES!

To help ensure that Sammy, his friends, and all the elements of our natural world can continue their journey in the precious life cycle that interconnects us all, a portion of the proceeds of this book with be donated to organizations that work to prevent and reverse the effects of global warming.